DON'T BRING YOUR DRAGON
TO THE LIBRARY

WRITTEN BY JULIE GASSMAN
ILLUSTRATED BY ANDY ELKERTON

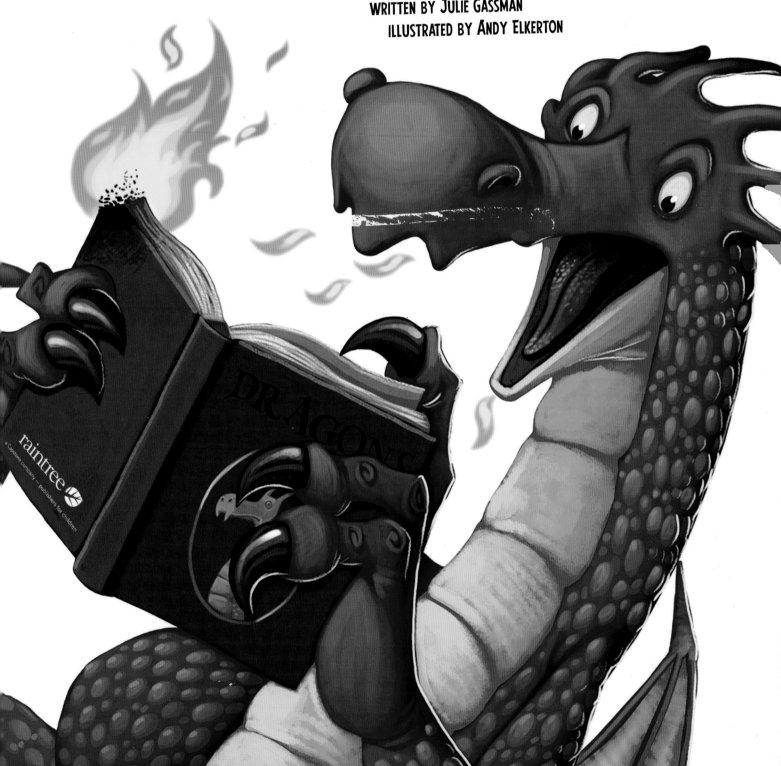

When you visit the library, please keep in mind:
no running, no shouting — to all books, be kind.

But there's one rule that's **bigger** than the rest.
And it **must** be followed by all of our guests . . .

A dragon is sometimes a very rude beast.
At story time he'll take up ten spaces, at least!

A dragon's big bottom can pack a real punch.
Each time he sits down, you'll hear a great CRUNCH!

You may ask her to come to a library show.
But trouble will start with the first song she knows.

Her swaying hips will crowd your space
with a dragon jig that has no grace.

SO DO **NOT** BRING YOUR DRAGON TO THE LIBRARY!

Maybe you're thinking, "Don't worry, it's fine.
There's plenty of space in that library of mine."

Perhaps that's true, but he's sure to roam.
Then you'll be wishing you had left him at home.

DRAGON TO THE LIBRARY!

You see, aisles of books are hard to resist.
She's sure to find sections that cannot be missed.

As she starts to read, she could overexcite,
and then chances are, her flame will **ignite!**

FAIRYTALES

I know, I know. What you're saying is true.
But leaving him at home will make me quite blue.

It's my favourite place. **Please**, listen to me.
My dragon would **love** our library!

Movies and computers and places to read.
Tales of heroes and adventure, of good and of greed.

Cookbooks and bios – oh, listen to my plea . . .

I'm afraid, my kind friend, I cannot agree.
A dragon in the library? It simply can't be.

But don't fret, don't frown. I have a solution.
Listen now to my smart substitution.

Your dragon should **not** miss the library treasures.
Just take home some books for her reading pleasure!

If you use your card often, you will very soon see . . .

... THAT YOU **NEVER** HAVE TO BRING YOUR DRAGON TO THE LIBRARY.

A special thanks to Sam for wisely suggesting that one should not bring dragons to the library, and to Anissa for sharing that bit of advice with me. -JG

ABOUT THE AUTHOR

The youngest in a family of nine children, Julie Gassman grew up in South Dakota, US. After college, she traded in small-town life for the world of magazine publishing in New York City. She now lives in southern Minnesota with her husband and their three children. No matter where she has lived, the public library has always been a special place for Julie, but she would never dream of bringing her pet dragon there.

ABOUT THE ILLUSTRATOR

After fourteen years as a graphic designer, Andy decided to go back to his illustrative roots as a children's book illustrator. Since 2002 he has produced work for picture books, educational books, advertising and toy design. Andy has worked for clients all over the world. He currently lives in a small tourist town on the west coast of Scotland with his wife and three children.

Raintree is an imprint of Capstone Global Library Limited, a company incorporated in England and Wales having its registered office at 264 Banbury Road, Oxford, OX2 7DY – Registered company number: 6695582

www.raintree.co.uk
myorders@raintree.co.uk

Text © Capstone Global Library Limited 2017
The moral rights of the proprietor have been asserted.

Printed and bound in China

ISBN: 978-1-474-72904-8

20 19 18 17 16
10 9 8 7 6 5 4 3 2 1

British Library Cataloguing in Publication Data
A full catalogue record for this book is available from the British Library.